Two Dads Are Better Than One

BY:

K.C. ECKELS

Library of Congress Control Number: 2015912317

CreateSpace Independent Publishing Platform, North Charleston, SC.

ISBN-13: 978-1515085621

ISBN-10: 1515085627

Printed in the United States of America

TEXT DESIGN BY K.C ECKELS
COVER DESIGN BY K.C. ECKELS
ARTWORK BY K.C. ECKELS

First Paperback Edition

This is for everyone who won the fight for marriage equality

My name is Suzie,

And I have two Dads,

They love me a lot,

And that makes me glad.

When people are mean,

That makes me sad,

They don't understand,

The family I have!

You can see for yourself,
That my family is great!
We go to the park,
And have lots of play dates!

On my first day of school,

I was really scared,

But my Daddies made it better,

By just being there!

For my birthday this year,
I had a party with friends!
I got a lot of great gifts,
But the best one was Fred!
(He's a hamster)

My Daddies got married,
It was a very special day,
I got to throw flowers,
And stay up real late!

My Dads are the best,

It really is true!

Just last week,

We went to the zoo!

We saw a monkey,
Just hanging around,
While on a train ride,
That went underground!

In the summer my Daddies,

Take me to the pool,

We splash and we swim,

So we can stay cool.

They let me play dress up,
Sometimes they play too,
I pretend we are robots,
That beep and say boo!

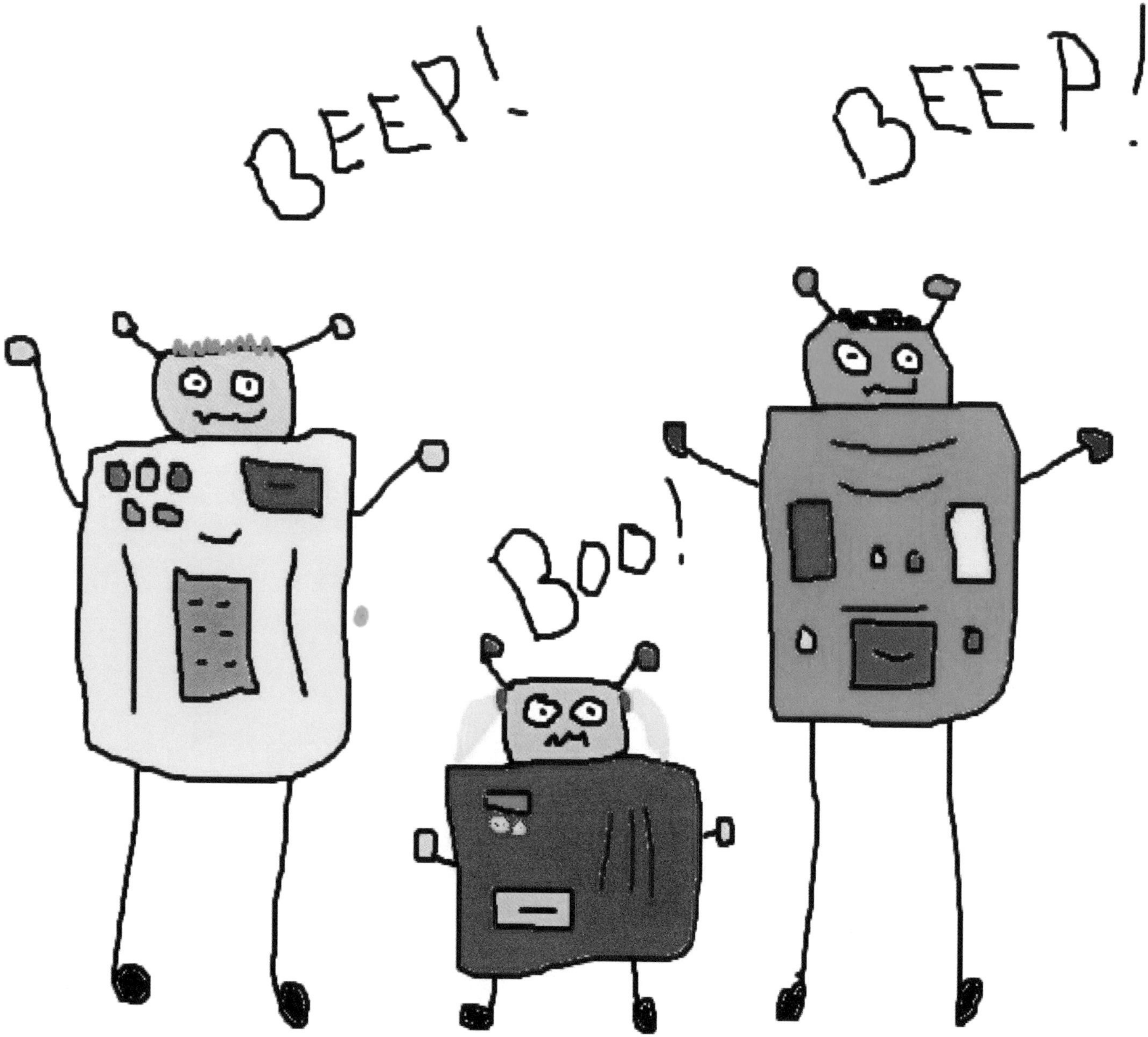
BEEP!
BOO!
BEEP!

We have family dinners,
At six every day,
We sit at the table,
Give thanks and pray.

Sometimes after dinner,

My Dads give me a treat!

Ice cream and cookies,

For dessert is neat!

After we eat,
I have to do chores,
I clean Fred's cage,
And put clothes in my drawers.

My Room

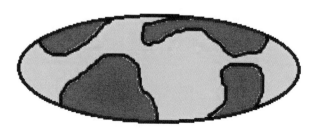

Right before sleep time,
I lay in my bed,
My Dads read me stories,
And then kiss my head.

STORY TIME

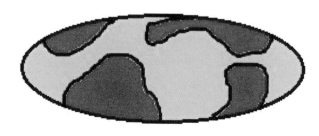

Having two Dads,

Is so much fun!

I would not want to know,

What it's like to have only one!

All families are different,
But yet still the same,
And if you judge someone,
That's just a shame.

This is my story,
And I'm happy to share,
My wonderful family,
With everyone, everywhere.

MY FAMILY

HIS FAMILY

THEIR FAMILY

YOUR FAMILY

Made in the USA
Lexington, KY
15 June 2016